MURDER IN THE CEMETERY

HAWK THERIOT & KRISTI BLOCKER SHORT STORIES BOOK 2

JIM RILEY

To the Most Beautiful

You Always Were and Always Will Be

1

Trouble was known to find the twins. Tonight was no exception.

"Are you sure?" Mindy asked.

"Have I ever lied to you?" her twin sister, Mandy, answered with her own question.

"How about when you told me I could trust Billy Bob on a date?"

"That doesn't count," Mandy countered. "You wore a see-through blouse."

"And you told me that escargot was French for boogers."

"Snails are a lot like boogers. That wasn't a lie."

"You're right," Mindy sighed. "They tasted like boogers."

"So when I tell you we'll find ghosts at the cemetery, believe me."

The twins pushed the ancient gate to the Morgan City cemetery open four inches. They only required that much room to squeeze their slim bodies inside. Both stood still, afraid to move among the burial plots.

"Why would a ghost come here?" Mindy asked.

"Billy Bob told me they like funerals," Mandy answered. "He wouldn't tell me why."

"He's the one that told me we had to get naked to see the drive-in movie. I guess he was right, though. Everybody around us took their clothes off."

"See. If he was right about that, he has to be right about the ghosts being here."

"The last time we went looking for ghosts, we found a dead man. Do you remember?"

"How can I forget? But why would a dead man come to a cemetery?"

"Maybe he planned ahead. You know, some guys buy insurance." Mindy whispered.

"Ghosts don't need insurance. They don't own anything except a sheet."

"Where do we go to find a ghost in here?"

"Follow me," Mandy said.

She took her twin's hand and led Mindy through the maze of graves. Moss hung from the century-old live oaks. With a slight wind, the moon blinked through a fine mist. Before long, the girls wrapped their arms around each other. An owl hooted overhead, causing both to shudder.

"I don't see any ghosts," Mindy said.

"Maybe it's like the drive-in. Maybe we have to take our clothes off to see one."

"But it's sprinkling. I don't like getting wet."

"Do you want to see a ghost?" Mandy asked.

"Duh." Mindy slapped the side of her head.

"Then we gotta do what we gotta do."

Mandy began undoing her blouse. Mindy followed. When the girls sat to untie their shoes, a huge swamp rat ran over their legs. As one, they leapt to their feet and ran headlong through the graveyard. Side by side, they tumbled into the open grave. Mindy screamed first. Mandy screamed louder.

"Yuck." Mindy whined. "When did they stop putting bodies in caskets?"

"I don't know, but we'd better go see Hawk. He'll know what to do."

2

HAWK THERIOT, THE ONLY FEDERAL RANGER ASSIGNED TO
the vast Atchafalaya Basin, stroked the knife on the whetstone
one final time. He rose to put in back in the cabinet when his
front door rattled. Accustomed to emergency late-night calls,
the ranger held onto the knife while rushing to the door. Four
little hands kept banging on it until he twisted the knob.

"I've got a doorbell," he began. "Why—?"

The sight of the twins standing on his front porch interrupted all thought. Especially with them wearing nothing
above the waist and blood dripping off their rust-colored hair.

"What the—?"

"C'mon, Ranger." Mandy grinned. "You've seen boobs
before. Don't get shy now."

"Just when I thought life was almost normal again," Hawk
muttered.

He had a habit of shaking his head when addressing the
twins.

"Come in before you catch pneumonia."

The girls pushed past the ranger without taking their gaze
off his physique.

"Want to take a shower with us?" Mandy asked. "We need to get this blood off."

"Not a good idea," Hawk replied.

"C'mon," Mindy said. "We have fun in the shower."

"I have no doubts," Hawk chuckled. "I think Kristi needs to see you before you destroy evidence."

"But we don't want to take a shower with Kristi," Mandy moaned. "We want to take a shower with you."

"Kristi is the sheriff. With that much blood, someone is dead or close to it."

"Duh," Mandy said. "Why else would he be in a grave?"

"I didn't know he was. How did you guys find a guy bleeding in a grave?"

"You don't keep up, do you?" Mindy asked. "If we found him in a grave, we had to be in the grave."

"And to be in the grave, we had to be in the graveyard," Mandy added.

Hawk shook his head again. "Why didn't I think of that?"

"That's why you have us," Mindy said. "We'll do the thinking for you."

Hawk stifled a groan.

"While you guys are here thinking for me, call Kristi. And don't wash until she gets here."

"Where are you going?" Mandy asked.

"Back to the graveyard to see what trouble you two have gotten into tonight."

3

HAWK HAD NO TROUBLE FINDING THE OPEN GRAVE. Stevie Wonder could have followed the path of destruction left by the scared twins. Flowers, once pristine at the foot of the graves, littered a four-foot wide tale of sheer panic. A stampede of cattle would not have caused as much damage.

The ranger found their blouses ten feet inside the gate. Neither had blood stains. He gathered them and followed the debris to the edge of the grave. Hawk laid the clothes to the side and squatted. In his experience, the ranger had seen too many investigators, deputies, and technicians spoil a crime scene by trampling on the evidence.

With the bright moon, the Swamp Ranger needed no flashlight. He preferred to see things in their natural element. A light made him focus only on the area within its beam. Slowly pivoting, he put together the scene.

The twins had meandered to the grave. They left on a more direct route, straight to the gate. Their long strides told the ranger they departed in a hurry. Hawk focused on the other sets of tracks. These made deeper impressions in the soft cemetery earth.

Hawk studied the signs left behind by all four individuals. Four people entered the graveyard. Three left. The twins made two of the exiting trails. A heavier person made the other. The ranger judged that a man between two hundred twenty and two hundred forty pounds walked out of the gate before the twins flew through it. He estimated the man's height at six-feet-two-inches by his stride.

On the way in, the large man had followed the fourth individual. Hawk knew this because the big man's tracks overlapped those of his smaller companion. The twin's tracks covered some of his, thus telling him they had come later.

He turned his attention to the man that made the fourth set of tracks. The one that lay dead in the grave. The ranger leaned forward and peered into the open hole. He found no joy in seeing the expected. A man less than six feet long looked like an eerie abstract painting in the moonlight. Blood streaked the body and the sides and bottom of the grave. Though the twins covered themselves with the red stains, they left plenty behind.

A third party observer may have concluded that the ranger froze in the position. For over twenty minutes, he did not move. Hawk knew this was his only chance to get a pristine view of the crime scene. He did not want to waste it.

Sirens interrupted his study. A squad car, lights flashing and siren blasting, lurched to a stop in front of the gate. Another followed only seconds later. Four deputies, with guns drawn, cautiously approached the cemetery.

"Hold on, fellows," Hawk said, without rising or turning. "Don't shoot me."

"Is that you, Hawk?" a familiar voice asked.

"Yep. And so far, I'm still alive. I'd like to keep it that way, Deputy Martin."

"It's okay," Martin said to the other deputies. "It's only Hawk."

"Seal the perimeter, Martin. Keep it that way until the techs get here. I'm coming out."

The ranger had all the information he needed to begin the investigation. It would start in the place he dreaded most, with an interview with the twins.

4

A FAMILIAR AROMA GREETED THE RANGER WHEN HE entered his camp.

"Who ordered pizza?" he called out.

"We had to eat," Sheriff Kristi Blocker replied. "Did you expect us to starve?"

"No chance of that happening with you around," Hawk chuckled.

In the kitchen, he found all three girls. He also found four empty pizza boxes. A quick glance told him the twins had eaten half a slice of Italian pie each. The portions did not surprise the ranger. Mindy and Mandy rarely ate. When they did, the twins picked at their food rather than consume it.

On the other hand, Kristi inhaled calories like a vacuum cleaner. Yet, the petite sheriff could have posed as a poster child for malnutrition. No matter how much food she gobbled, the slim officer never gained an ounce. That fact did not deter her from trying. For her to eat four pizzas compared to the twins eating a green salad. A small one shared between both.

"What did you find?" Kristi asked while examining a slice of pepperoni pie.

"Just what I expected," Hawk replied. "Once again, the twins left a dead body in their wake."

"It's not our fault," Mandy whined.

"That's right," Mindy added. "I mean, who would expect to find a dead body in a grave?"

"What did you expect to find?"

"Ghosts, you silly goose," Mandy said.

"Billy Bob told us that was the only place to see a real ghost," Mindy chimed.

"Did he also tell you to take your blouses off?" Hawk asked.

"No, silly." Mandy replied.

"He told us to get naked," Mindy said. "He said it was the best way to get lucky."

Hawk groaned and turned to Kristi.

"You need to have a long talk with these two and explain to them that Billy Bob is more concerned with his own luck than theirs."

Kristi grinned and stuffed a slice of meat lover's pizza in her mouth. Hawk turned back to the twins.

"Did either of you recognize the victim?"

"I did," Mandy said.

"Me, too." Mindy echoed.

"Who is he?"

"The dead man in the grave," both said at once.

5

THE TWINS WERE UNSEEN, BUT NOT UNHEARD WHEN Kristi greeted Hawk at the door. The teenagers jabbered away in a bedroom.

"What did you find?" Kristi asked, giving Hawk a tight hug.

"Those two," Hawk pointed in the direction of the twin's voices, "really messed up the crime scene. I hope your techs can recover enough evidence to help."

"That bad, huh?"

"Worse," Hawk sighed. "But I picked up a few things."

"Like what?"

"The killer is between six-three and six-four. Weighs about two hundred forty pounds. Slight limp in his left leg. Knows how to use a knife."

"You found a witness?" Kristi's eyes grew wide.

"Just what I could pick up from the few signs the twins didn't destroy."

"You said they wrecked the scene. How did you come up with all that?"

"Blind luck," Hawk laughed. "I found a few tracks they missed in the mayhem."

"Are you sure you didn't peek at a security video? How can you tell all that from a few tracks?"

"Because he's the Swamp Ranger," Mandy giggled as the twins entered.

"He can track a fart through a hurricane," Mindy added.

"Remind me to cover my tracks the next time I run away from home," Kristi smiled.

"You're leaving?" Mandy arched her eyebrows.

"Can we keep Hawk after you leave?" Mindy asked.

"I'm just pulling his chain," Kristi explained.

"I'd like to pull something of his." Mandy edged close to Hawk.

"Me too," Mindy moved to the ranger's other side.

Hawk tossed the blouses from the graveyard to the girls.

"They didn't need these for evidence since they found no blood on them."

Both began unbuttoning the tops Kristi loaned them.

"Do that in the bedroom," the petite sheriff ordered.

"Why? Hawk saw our boobs earlier," Mandy said.

"And he smiled when he did," Mindy giggled.

"He'll like them a lot less with me here," Kristi shot a glance at the tall ranger. Then she turned back to the twins. "Now off to the bedroom."

The girls walked toward the hallway. When Kristi turned back to Hawk, Mandy and Mindy stopped and grinned at Hawk. Then they flashed their tiny breasts before disappearing.

Hawk strained to keep a straight face while Kristi lectured about his bad influence on the youngsters. That effort was almost too much.

"They're just babies, Hawk. How can you encourage them like that?"

"I didn't encourage them," Hawk shrugged. "Though I've never known them to need much."

"Well, you don't have to enjoy their antics like you do. I've got to check on the crime scene."

Kristi slammed the door on her way to log in at the graveyard, leaving Hawk with the twins. Knowing nothing good could come of his time with those two, the ranger left in search of the killer.

6

Hawk found the abandoned pickup truck at the third parking lot. The tracks left at the graveyard told him both men had arrived in the same vehicle. The ranger figured the victim rode to the cemetery in the killer's car. Adding the strong aroma of alcohol coming off the corpse, he concluded the extra vehicle was probably at a bar.

At the Teche Lights Out Bar, Hawk spotted the decade-old blue F150 alone in the parking lot. Because it was an hour before daylight, he did not expect any other vehicles. He pulled the black F-250 alongside and exited his favorite truck.

Finding the doors unlocked, he started on the passenger side. He did not bother calling in for a warrant because he was certain the truck's owner was dead. The vehicle was part of the crime scene, and he needed to search it to find the killer.

The registration showed that the pickup belonged to Adrian Frazell. When alive, Mr. Frazell lived on Hospital Drive in Morgan City. Hawk jotted down the information and replaced the documents. A search under the passenger seat revealed nothing of interest.

He worked around the bed, stopping with each step to

examine minute details. A brown stain on the bumper caught his attention. Closer inspection showed it was a spot of old blood, too old to be relevant to the murder. Shaking his head, Hawk extended the search.

Hawk discovered the most pertinent clue on the lot outside the driver's side door. Four huge drops of fresh blood. Dry on the edges, but mushy in the centers. This is where the killer abducted Frazell, leading to the execution at the cemetery.

Two yards away, the ranger spotted a shoe print identical to the ones at the graveyard.

This put the killer both at the bar and at the point of death. He took pictures of the blood and the prints before curious onlookers or over-eager technicians obliterated them.

He first felt a brief spurt of exhilaration over his progress. Then a glance at the closed bar dampened his enthusiasm. There were no witnesses to interview until the bar opened later in the day. A lot could happen in the interim.

7

"Do you think Hawk will marry Kristi?" Mandy asked, a finger twirling strands of rust-colored hair.

"I hope not," Mindy mimicked her sister's hair twirling. "I hope he marries us."

"Us? I don't think that's legal here. We'd have to move to Utah or Saudi Arabia."

"Then we'll kidnap him and take him to Utah," Mindy said.

"That's a long way to drive. It's past Shreveport, I think."

"Then well drive to Saudi Arabia," Mindy proclaimed. "Is it closer than Shreveport?"

"Billy Bob went there once. I think it's on the other side of Baton Rouge, but he was too busy to make much sense."

"I know how busy Billy Bob can be. If he was talking during that, he probably wasn't telling the truth."

"I bet Kristi won't be happy if we take Hawk away from Morgan City. What will we do about her?" Mandy asked.

"Let's tell her," Mindy beamed. "She's our friend. If she lets Hawk go with us, he can make two people happy instead of one."

"Would you let Hawk go if you were Kristi?"

Mindy hesitated. Before she could reply, a window leading to the rear porch shattered. The twins, always in search of adventure, ran toward the sound.

"Who are you?" Mandy asked.

Why did you break the window?" Mindy followed before the man could issue an answer.

He had a crude, almost vulgar look to him. Twice the size of the girls, his bloodshot eyes glared at the twins. Spittle dripped onto a scraggly beard. A dragon tattoo stretched from under a stained shirt to his right ear.

None of those features bothered the twins. The other one did. All four of their eyes focused on the twelve-inch blade he held.

"Have you told anyone?" the big goon slurred.

"Told anyone what?" Mandy asked.

"We tell everything we know and some things we don't," Mindy added. "We're gonna tell Hawk that you broke his window."

"Ya'll didn't tell him I was at the graveyard?" The man lifted the long knife.

"How could we?" Mandy asked.

"We didn't see you there," Mindy said.

"You ran right by me and my truck. How could you have missed me?"

"We were looking for ghosts," Mandy said.

"And you aren't a ghost," Mindy added.

"You two are about to be," the thug took a menacing step toward them, brandishing the blade.

"If you hurt us, Hawk will get mad," Mandy said.

"And you don't want to make Hawk mad," Mindy added.

The ugly man laughed. An ugly laugh that caused the twins to shudder. They took a step back. For the first time, they understood the peril of the situation. They glanced at each other, communicating in a way that only twins can.

The goon lowered his head like a bull and charged, the knife slashing out in front of his body. The steel blade hit nothing but air. When he looked up after passing the spot the twins had been, he saw nothing of them. They vanished. His jaw dropped. More drool spilled onto the scraggly beard.

Cursing, he left Hawk's camp. Another target was added to his list. Not only did he have to eliminate the twins, he would have to kill the federal ranger.

8

"CAN YA'LL DESCRIBE HIM?"

Hawk questioned the twins after the search of the Frazell residence turned up little to help. He found that the deceased gambled before meeting his demise. Cheat sheets and racing forms sprinkled the tops of tables and furniture throughout the house.

Frazell had been a roughneck, providing brute labor on a rig in the Gulf of Mexico on a seven-on-seven-off rotation. When the pool of contractors got tight, he often switched to working fourteen days in between seven day breaks. For an unskilled high school dropout, he made good money.

The problem arose with the seven days onshore. Like many of his coworkers, Frazell spent leisure time drinking and gambling. And like many, he ran up debts he struggled to pay. From the evidence, Hawk deduced Frazell enjoyed Texas Hold-'em and betting on the ponies. He mastered neither.

After returning, Hawk found the broken window. He also found the twins hiding under the kitchen table, clinging to the underside beneath the cloth. Both talked rapidly. At the same time. For over ten minutes, the ranger tried to calm the excited girls enough to answer his questions. As always, the twins added to the mystery.

"He was twelve feet tall," Mandy gushed.

"No, he wasn't." Mindy said. "He was only ten feet. Maybe eleven."

"And he was six feet wide." Mandy ignored her sister's correction.

"That part is true," Mindy nodded.

"His beard hung down to his knees," Mandy said.

"It was purple and red," Mindy exclaimed.

"And the sword was at least nine feet long." Mandy stretched her slim arms as wide as possible.

"It had blood dripping from it," Mindy grimaced."

"What did he say?" Hawk asked, not bothering to take notes.

"He was hard to understand," Mandy said.

"Like he was talking through one of those boxes," Mindy nodded.

Hawk groaned. With these two as eyewitnesses, he would not get a jury to convict a banana of being yellow. Not that the twins had any peers to serve on the panel. They were in a world of their own. One that he did not understand.

"Did he say anything about the murder at the graveyard?"

"He saw us, but we didn't see him," Mandy said.

"That's how we know he was lying," Mindy shook her rust-colored mane. "Cause he looked like a ghost and we were looking for ghosts."

"Would you recognize him if you saw him again?" Hawk asked.

Both twins nodded. Hawk was not so sure. If a twelve-foot man had been walking around the streets of Morgan City, he would have noticed. Little did he know that he was about to get a much better description.

9

KRISTI SIGHED. A LONG, DEEP EXHALATION. SHE DID NOT enjoy crime scenes, especially when they had bloody bodies. And this one had one. Adrian Frazell had not been handsome in life. He did not improve in death.

The deep knife wound slashed through half of his back. It allowed Frazell to thrash around in the grave enough to cast blood stains in every direction. But the more the petite sheriff looked around, the more puzzled she became.

Hawk told her that the man used a knife. However, the techs had not moved the body by the time the sheriff arrived. The corpse laid face-up in the grave. The long gash could not be seen from above. How did Hawk know someone stabbed him?

She also searched for the tracks he saw that described the killer. Kristi got down on her hands and knees, looking for the revealing signs. She could not find any. When she asked the technicians, they could only shrug. None of them saw anything remarkable in the dirt except for the trail left by the twins.

The medical examiner arrived and took pictures of the

body in place. Then, with the help of the technicians, they loaded it on a gurney and moved it to the waiting wagon. The two deputies followed the wagon back into town, leaving the small sheriff alone in the cemetery.

The flashlight seemed small without the others around. Shivers went up Kristi's back when an owl hooted. Two mice scurried to make a meal of the spilled blood. Another sound startled the small lady. It did not come from nature. The sound emanated from a human. Almost a cough, but not quite.

Kristi's eyes darted back and forth, trying to pierce the darkness. The beam of the flashlight did not extend far enough to capture the source. The sheriff drew the Smith & Wesson .38 revolver and pointed it at the blackness.

"Who's there?" she asked, her voice breaking

Silence.

"I've got a gun. Who is there?" she asked again.

As if on cue, the owl flapped its great wings and flew right over the sheriff's head. Kristi ducked and only great discipline prevented her from firing the gun.

When she turned, the owl had one mouse in its talons. The other rodent scurried away, figuring the cost of dinner was too expensive to stick around.

Kristi chided herself for being such a baby. There was nothing to be afraid of among the dead bodies. None would rise from the grave and attack her. She holstered the weapon.

She felt the point of the knife in the middle of her back. She knew she was in trouble.

10

"I'VE GOT YOUR BITCH," THE GRAVELLY VOICE CAME OVER the phone.

"Who is this?" Hawk asked.

"I'm the guy that's gonna kill your girlfriend unless you do what I want."

"How do I know you have Kristi?" Hawk asked.

"Maybe this will convince you."

The scream caused the ranger's knees to buckle. He had no doubt the terrorized voice belonged to Kristi. He loved that voice under different circumstances. He loved the person who owned it even more.

Hawk inhaled, trying to calm his excited nerves. His hand squeezed the cell so tight, it almost broke. His jaws clenched so hard, the sides of his head pounded.

"What is it?" Mandy asked.

"Is Kristi in trouble?"

Hawk ignored the twins, concentrating on the gravelly voice.

"Where is she?" Hawk asked.

"I'll tell you after you agree to the deal," came the reply.

"I don't deal with vermin," Hawk said. "I kill them."

"You gotta deal with me if you ever want to see this bitch again."

"If you harm her in any way, I will kill you. But first, I'll make you beg for death," Hawk whispered.

"Big talk when I'm holding a royal flush," the man spat over the cell. "I've got your bitch, and that's the biggest card in the deck."

"I'll come to you." Hawk did not recognize the sound of his own voice. He had faced death many times. It was not the same as knowing Kristi's life hung in the balance of his decisions. "You can take me and let Kristi go."

"I'll take you. I also want those two skinny bitches that saw me at the graveyard."

"The twins?" Hawk blurted before realizing both were within arm's reach.

"That's them. Look exactly alike. Talk alike, too."

"I can't. You'll have to deal with me."

Another scream. This one even more shrill. Hawk cringed at the sound. He felt two delicate hands on his forearm.

"He wants us, doesn't he?" Mandy asked.

"We'll go," Mindy added.

Hawk shook his head.

"Is that them yakking behind you?" the voice asked.

"It's them," Hawk replied. "But you will get nowhere near them again."

"I will unless you want your little girl here to find out how a real man does it."

Hawk felt the bile rise in his throat. The small hands on his forearm tightened. He turned and saw two smiling faces. He knew what he had to do.

"Okay," he said. "Where can I find you and Kristi?"

"At the cemetery. I believe you know the way."

The silence on the other end of the line was the loudest Hawk had ever heard.

11

When Hawk got out of his truck, his heart raced like never before. A gray mist floated over the graveyard like a thin blanket. The local owl announced his arrival.

The ranger walked through the open gate and stopped. He did not want to rush into a trap. Hawk did not pull the familiar .357 revolver. Instead, his fingers rested on its handle.

"Back here," the same gravelly voice called from the back of the cemetery.

Hawk had no flashlight. He needed none. The ranger learned long ago to let his eyes adjust to the darkness. He saw the big, ugly man standing close to the back fence with a rope in his hand. The ranger's gaze followed the rope's path. It stretched to the bough of an ancient live oak about ten feet above the ground. The taut cord went under the bough and tied to a rickety chair.

On top of the chair stood the petite sheriff, her tiny toes stretching up as far as possible. Around Kristi's neck was a noose; it's other end tied to the ancient bough. Hawk felt his own knees buckle at her distress. The panicked look was almost too much for him to take.

"C'mon in and join the party," the gravelly voice said.

Hawk took a step forward, first inspecting the ground before him.

"Don't be scared," the voice taunted. "Where are those two bitches?"

"They're just down the road," Hawk lied. He had argued with Mandy and Mindy for over twenty minutes before they agreed to stay at his camp until this was over.

"Why are they down the road? I need them here."

"They'll come as soon as Kristi is safe. Not before."

"That won't work," the ugly man said.

"It'll have to," Hawk replied. "I won't put them in danger until I have Kristi."

"Ain't gonna work. I'll take your little bitch and have some fun with her. Then I'll find the other two on my own."

"I can't let you do that," Hawk said. "She's staying here with me."

"The only way she stays here is if she's as dead as everyone else here. You can't see her in the dark, but she can't get away without killing herself."

Even in daylight, the man at the rear of the cemetery probably would not have seen Hawk's hand flash. He might have seen the knife rocket through the air like a guided missile straight to its target. The sharp blade severed the cord between Kristi's neck and the bough. He saw two thin shapes grab the small sheriff and ease her off the ground.

He rolled his eyes at the twins. They had not stayed at his camp. Although he should not have been surprised. They never listened to him before.

He turned his attention back to the man with the gravelly voice. The one holding a twelve-inch blade.

12

THE THUG HAD NO IDEA THAT HE NO LONGER HAD KRISTI as a hostage. The rope he held taut remained tied to the empty chair.

"You can leave, Ranger," the man said. "I'll leave the bitch's body here for you to find tomorrow. Unless you want to give me those girls."

Hawk said nothing. He was already halfway to the man without making a sound.

"C'mon, ranger. Let's make a deal. I'd hate to have to kill your skinny girlfriend."

Hawk froze ten feet from the man. He retrieved an ink pen and tossed it in the darkness over the man's head. When it hit a headstone, the thug jerked around, pulling the rope with him. The empty chair clattered toward them.

Hawk kicked, breaking the wrist less than an inch from the knife handle. The thug screamed in surprise and pain. His knife flew harmlessly through the air.

Hawk's rage overpowered his restraint. He had no idea how long he pummeled the helpless thug before a soft hand grabbed his arm.

"That's enough," Kristi said in a soft feminine tone. "If you kill him, we'll be at the office for hours filling out the paperwork."

"It'll be worth it," Hawk rasped. "I'm not in any hurry."

"I am," Kristi laughed. "Almost getting hanged made me hungry."

NOTES

Murder in the Cemetery is a short story in the Hawk Theriot and Kristi Blockers series. It features the dynamic duo with even greater challenges.

I have taken great literary license with the geography and data of Morgan City. They are wonderful and a great way to experience the Cajun culture. I lived there for over four years and found it to be one of the most desirable places on earth if you enjoy the outdoors, great cuisine and remarkable people.

There are so many people to thank:

My family, Linda, Josh, Dalton & Jade

David and Sara Sue

C D and Debbie Smith

My brother and sister-in-law, Bill & Pam

My sister, Debbie

My sister-in-law and her husband, Brenda & Jerry

The Sunday School class at Zoar Baptists

Any and all mistakes, typos and errors are my fault and mine alone. If you would like to get in touch with me, go to my web site at http://jimrileyweb.wix.com/jimrileybooks.

I thank you for reading **_Murder in the Cemetery_** and hope you will also enjoy the rest my books.

Dear reader,

We hope you enjoyed reading *Murder in the Cemetery*. Please take a moment to leave a review, even if it's a short one. Your opinion is important to us.

Discover more books by Jim Riley at

https://www.nextchapter.pub/authors/jim-riley

Want to know when one of our books is free or discounted? Join the newsletter at

http://eepurl.com/bqqB3H

Best regards,

Jim Riley and the Next Chapter Team

9 781034 502265